...AND BETWEEN THESE TWO CONTINENTS IS THE ATLANTIC OCEAN.

Editorial Director: FRANÇOISE MOULY · Managing Editor: SASHA STEINBERG · Book Design: FRANÇOISE MOULY

Hand-lettering: MYKEN BOMBERGER & FRED · FRED'S artwork was drawn in India ink, watercolor, and gouache.

ABDOPUBLISHING.COM

Reinforced library bound edition published in 2017 by Spotlight, a division of ABDO, PO Box 398166, Minneapolis, Minnesota 55439. Spotlight produces high-quality reinforced library bound editions for schools and libraries. Published by agreement with TOON Books.

Printed in the United States of America, North Mankato, Minnesota.
042016
092016

THIS BOOK CONTAINS
RECYCLED MATERIALS

FOR VISUAL READERS
TOON
GRAPHICS

WWW.TOON-BOOKS.COM

LIBRARY OF CONGRESS CATALOGING-IN-PUBLICATION DATA

This book was previously cataloged with the following information:

Fred, 1931- author, illustrator. [Philémon et le château suspendu. English]
 The suspended castle : a Philemon adventure : a TOON graphic / by Fred ; translated by Richard Kutner.
 pages cm. – (TOON Graphics)
Originally published by Dargaud in 1973 under title: Philémon et le château suspendu.
Summary: "Philemon and his friend Mr. Bartholomew journey back to the mysterious islands of the Atlantic, and discover an owl lighthouse, a ship that is also a whale, and a castle hanging from a string"-- Provided by publisher.
ISBN 978-1-935179-86-3 (hardcover)
1. Graphic novels. [1. Graphic novels. 2. Adventure and adventurers--Fiction. 3. Islands--Fiction. 4. Comics & Graphic Novels / General.--Juvenile fiction. 5. Fantasy & Magic.--Juvenile fiction. 6. Humorous Stories.--Juvenile fiction. 7. Action & Adventure / General.--Juvenile fiction.] I. Kutner, Richard, translator. II. Title.
PZ7.7.F73 Su 2015
741.5'944--dc23
                    2015003940

ISBN 978-1-61479-501-8 (reinforced library bound edition)

Spotlight
A Division of ABDO
abdopublishing.com

THE SUSPENDED CASTLE

A PHILEMON ADVENTURE

A TOON GRAPHIC BY

FRED

Translated by RICHARD KUTNER

MEET PHILEMON

PHILEMON IS AN IMAGINATIVE TEENAGER WHO LIVES ON A FARM IN FRANCE, BACK IN THE 1960S. WHEN A MESSAGE IN A BOTTLE SPARKS HIS CURIOSITY, HE FALLS RIGHT INTO A WORLD OF FANTASTIC ADVENTURES...

ANATOLE IS A DONKEY AND PHIL'S TRUSTY FRIEND. ANATOLE TRIES TO HELP PHIL STAY OUT OF TROUBLE, BUT PHIL'S ADVENTUROUS SPIRIT AND CURIOSITY GET THE BEST OF HIM.

HECTOR IS PHILEMON'S GROUCHY FATHER, WHO REFUSES TO BELIEVE PHIL'S WILD STORIES.

PHILEMON FALLS DOWN A WELL AND WAKES UP ON A STRANGE ISLAND IN THE MIDDLE OF THE ATLANTIC. THERE HE MEETS A WELL DIGGER, **MR. BARTHOLOMEW**, WHO LANDED THERE YEARS AGO. UNFORTUNATELY, THE TWO NEW FRIENDS ARE SEPARATED.

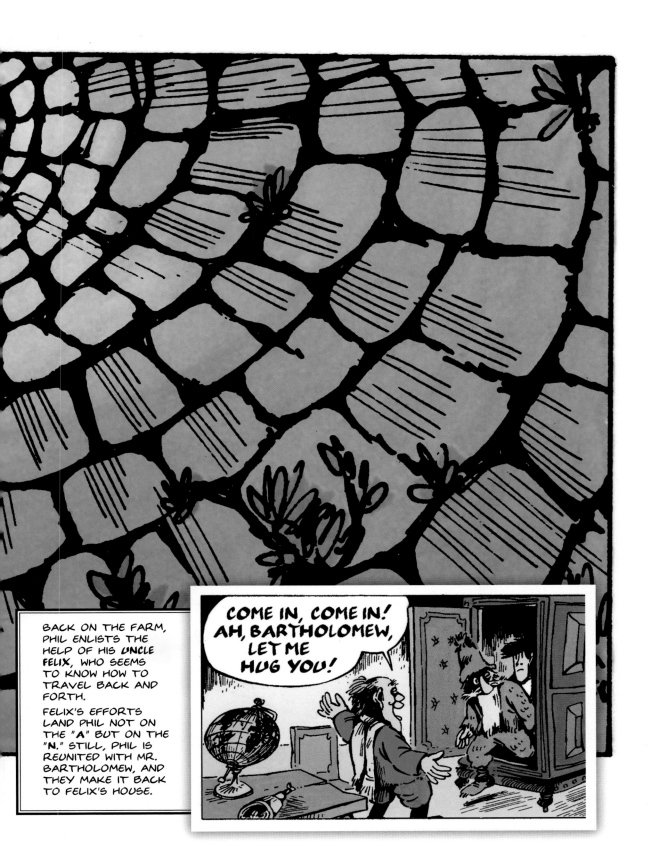

BACK ON THE FARM, PHIL ENLISTS THE HELP OF HIS **UNCLE FELIX,** WHO SEEMS TO KNOW HOW TO TRAVEL BACK AND FORTH.

FELIX'S EFFORTS LAND PHIL NOT ON THE "A" BUT ON THE "N." STILL, PHIL IS REUNITED WITH MR. BARTHOLOMEW, AND THEY MAKE IT BACK TO FELIX'S HOUSE.

COME IN, COME IN! AH, BARTHOLOMEW, LET ME HUG YOU!

BOO HOO
BOO HOO...

BOO HOO BOO HOO...
SNIFF!... SNIFF!... SNIFF!

HUH?

I GUESS MUSHROOMS
MAKE YOU SAD...

UH... MR. BARTHOLOMEW,
ARE YOU OK?

OH, HELLO, PHILEMON...
SNIFF!... SNIFF!

BOO HOO HOOOOO!
SNIFF!... SNIFF!...
BOO HOO HOO!

TELL ME, MR.
BARTHOLOMEW, WHAT'S
GOING ON? GET A HOLD
OF YOURSELF...

OH, MY GOODNESS!
MY OH MY!
MY
OH
MY!

I'M UNHAPPY, PHILEMON.
VERY UNHAPPY. SNIFF!... SNIFF!

SNUFFLE!

WELL, THAT'S
EASY TO SEE.
BUT WHY?

DON'T I LOOK RIDICULOUS
IN THESE CLOTHES?

WELL, MAYBE...

YOU REMEMBER HOW WELL
DRESSED I WAS ON THE "A"...?*

*SEE: CAST AWAY ON THE LETTER A

...AND FRIDAY...YOU REMEMBER
FRIDAY, DON'T YOU? NOW
THERE WAS A CENTAUR! AND
WHAT ABOUT MY CASTLE? MY
CASTLE...OH, MY GOODNESS!
OH MY, OH MY! SNIFF! SNIFF!
IT WAS WONDERFUL...

BUT... DON'T
TELL ME YOU'RE
HOMESICK FOR
THE "A"!

WELL,
PHILEMON,
I KNOW IT
SOUNDS
SILLY, BUT
I'M BORED
HERE.

YOU SEE, PHIL, I LIVED TOO MANY YEARS ON THE "A"... FORTY YEARS IS A LONG TIME—A VERY LONG TIME...

I CAN'T GET USED TO LIVING IN THIS WORLD. EVERYTHING IS STRANGE HERE... BOTTLES DON'T GROW ON TREES, THERE'S ONLY **ONE** SUN, PEOPLE WORK—THE LIST GOES ON AND ON!

OH, WHY DID I EVER SEND MESSAGES FROM THE "A"? I WAS SO HAPPY DOWN THERE... SO HAPPY... REALLY HAPPY... OH, MY... **SNIFF!**

HOLD ON, MR. BARTHOLOMEW, MAYBE THERE'S A WAY TO...

WHAT?

YOU THINK SO? YOU THINK THAT I COULD GO BACK DOWN THERE? YES? YOU THINK SO? TELL ME, DO YOU **REALLY** THINK SO?

THERE'S ONLY ONE PERSON WHO CAN TELL US IF IT'S POSSIBLE...

AS FOR ME, I'M GOING BACK HOME...

YES, YES, YES, YES, YES, YES, YES, YES...

A SHORT WHILE LATER, AT UNCLE FELIX'S HOUSE...

"Enfants Porteurs" Set
White marble base, finely gilt imitation bronze statuettes and ornaments.
14-6924 Mantel clock, height 13 in. Guaranteed ten years. Our price.......**$500**
14-6026 Matching vases, height 8 in. Our price............................**$220**

COME ON, BARTHOLOMEW, YOU HAVE TO MAKE A DECISION!

WHEN YOU'RE ON THE "A", YOU WANT TO LEAVE. WHEN YOU'RE **NOT** ON THE "A", YOU WANT TO GO **BACK**. I'M NOT A TRAVEL AGENT, YOU KNOW!

BOO HOO HOO BOOOOOO... SNIFF! SNIFF!

?

HMPH! OK, OK...LET ME SEE WHAT I CAN DO...

3

FOLLOW ME.

YOU'RE GOING TO GO BY WAY OF THE **SEASHELL**, BARTHOLOMEW.

THE SEASHELL?

YES. YOU CAN NEVER GO TO THE **"A"** OF THE ATLANTIC OCEAN THE SAME WAY TWICE—THAT WOULD BE TOO EASY! **EVERYBODY** WOULD GO THERE.

INFLATE THE...

HELP ME TO INFLATE THE SHELL, PHIL.

WHERE'S THE PUMP? **OH!** HERE IT IS.

CLINK! CLANK.

DO WHAT I TELL **YOU**.

OK, OK.

DESERTED ISLAND

ARE YOU SURE YOU WANT TO DO THIS, BARTHOLOMEW? **WHERE...**

INFLATE A SEASHELL—ONLY UNCLE FELIX COULD THINK OF THAT!

PFFFFFT PFFFFFT PFFFFT PFFFT

BUT WHERE DID BARTHOLOMEW GO?

PFFFFTT PFFFFTT FFFTT FF

15

THE DOT OF THE "**i**"? ARE YOU SURE?

SURE I'M SURE! WHAT'S WITH YOU? YOU WANT TO FIGHT?

IT JUST SO HAPPENS THAT I HAVE BEEN THE GUARDIAN-KING OF THE OWL-LIGHTHOUSE FOR 430 YEARS! SO **THERE**!

HMPH!

?

THE OWL-LIGHTHOUSE?

YES, THE OWL-LIGHTHOUSE, CELEBRATED IN SONG AND POETRY...

BURP!

...WERE IT NOT FOR THE OWL-LIGHTHOUSE ON THE DOT OF THE "**i**" OF THE ATLANTIC OCEAN, HOW MANY SAILORS, HOW MANY CAPTAINS WOULD HAVE LOST THEIR WAY ON THEIR JOURNEYS TO FAR-OFF LANDS?

OH, COME **ON**!

BURP!

SO, FELIX MESSED UP AGAIN! WE'RE NOT ON THE "**A**"...

IT'S BECOMING A HABIT WITH HIM!

HMPH!

THE "**A**"! THE "**A**"! IT'S ALL VERY FUNNY, THIS "**A**" BUSINESS!... LISTEN, THERE'S MORE TO LIFE THAN JUST THE "**A**"!

BUT I, UH, DON'T SEE ANY LIGHTHOUSE. WHERE IS YOUR OWL-LIGHTHOUSE?

SLURP, CHOMP, MUNCH!

THE OWL-LIGHTHOUSE APPEARS ONLY AT NIGHTFALL, OF COURSE. DON'T YOU KNOW **ANYTHING**?

BURP!

IN ANY CASE, IT SHOULD BE HERE SOON. THE SUNS ARE SETTING...

8

BE CAREFUL, PHIL!

I KNOW—BUT WHAT ELSE CAN WE DO?

HEY, IT'S **HOLLOW** INSIDE!

OF COURSE! AT NIGHT, ALL OWL-LIGHTHOUSES ARE HOLLOW! THESE TWO DON'T HAVE A **CLUE**!

WATCH YOUR STEP!

OUCH!

HOO HOO!

LOOK AT THE MAGNIFICENT VIEW FROM HERE.

ISN'T IT BEAUTIFUL? UNFORTUNATELY, NO SHIP EVER PASSES BY HERE... NO ONE, EVER. WELL, YOU CAN'T HAVE **EVERYTHING**...

I'VE BEEN THINKING... IF YOU REALLY WANT TO GO TO THE "A"...

HOO HOO!

...TAKE THE LUMINOUS PATHWAY.

THE **LUMINOUS PATHWAY**?

YES, THE LUMINOUS PATHWAY GOES STRAIGHT TO THE "A"! TAKE IT!

YOU MEAN THAT WE CAN WALK ON THE RAY OF LIGHT?

WELL, OF COURSE!

HOO HOO!

BUT YOU HAVE TO GET TO YOUR DESTINATION BEFORE DAWN, OR ELSE...

OR ELSE WHAT?

OR ELSE, SPLASH! THE OWL-LIGHTHOUSE TURNS OFF AND FLIES AWAY AT SUNRISE.

HMM... WHAT DO YOU THINK, PHIL?

WELL... IF IT'S THE ONLY WAY TO LEAVE THE DOT OF THE "i"...

WATCH OUT, PHIL!

AND REMEMBER! GET THERE BEFORE DAWN! YOU HAVE TO MAKE IT BEFORE DAWN...

OK, OK. WE'VE GOT IT!

HOO HOO!

IT'S ALL RIGHT, MR. BARTHOLOMEW— YOU CAN COME. IT WILL HOLD US UP.

HOO HOO!

HOO HOO!

HOO HOO!

HOO HOO!

HOO HOO!

THAT OWL-LIGHTHOUSE IS GETTING ON MY NERVES. I KEEP THINKING HE'S ASKING WHO WE ARE...

IT'S A STRANGE FEELING. THIS RAY OF LIGHT IS BOUNCY LIKE RUBBER...

PHILEMON!

?

QUICK! HURRY!

BETTER WATCH WHERE YOU'RE WALKING!

OOF!

IF YOU STEP OFF THE RAY OF LIGHT, YOU FALL. THAT'S OBVIOUS.

OBVIOUS... OBVIOUS...

HURRY UP, MR. BARTHOLOMEW. THE NIGHT WILL SOON BE OVER...

MY FEET HURT!

NO NEED TO RUN, PHIL. WE'LL NEVER MAKE IT!

?

LOOK—IT'S ALREADY DAWN!

OH!

22

GENTLY ROCKED BY THE OCEAN WAVES, THE WHALE-GALLEY DRIFTS OFF TO SLEEP BENEATH THE TWO MOONS.

INSIDE, THE CAPTAIN IS SNORING AS ONLY THE CAPTAIN OF A WHALE-GALLEY CAN...

ZZZZ ZZZZ ZZZ

ZZZZ ZZZZ ZZZ

SU-D-DEN-LY!

ALERT!

A MUTINY, CAPTAIN, A MUTINY!

WHAT ARE YOU TALKING ABOUT? A MU-MU-ON-MY-WH-WHALE—A MUTINY ON MY WHALE-GA-GA-GALLEY?

YES, CAPTAIN. IT'S A REVOLT BY THE PRISONERS!

WHAT'S GOING ON? CAN'T A DRAGON GET ANY SLEEP?

LET'S GO!

WE WON'T BE EXPLOITED ANYMORE!

DON'T PUSH!

TO THE DEATH!

DON'T PUSH!

THAT'S RIGHT!

ROW! DON'T PADDLE!

TO THE DEATH! ENOUGH!

ROW!

WHAT'S GOING ON?

COME WITH US! WE'RE GOING TO PUT AN END TO THIS!

ROW ROW ROW ROW ROW ROW ROW ROW ROW ROW

33

25

PHILEMON MUST BE TRAPPED IN THE WHALE-GALLEY, THE POOR BOY. SNIFF! SNIFF!

THE SUSPENDED CASTLE IS IN VIEW, CAPTAIN.

PREPARE TO DROP ANCHOR.

OOF!

SO, GUYS, WAS IT A GOOD CATCH?

BAH!

WE HARPOONED A WHALE-GALLEY, BUT IT WASN'T THE LEGAL SIZE, SO WE THREW IT BACK IN THE WATER...

HE LIES LIKE A FISHERMAN!

YEAH, RIGHT!

GET OFF THE RUNWAY!

HEY, LET ME CATCH MY BREATH.

GO!

OH WELL! IT LOOKS LIKE WE WON'T BE EATING ANY WHALE-GALLEY MEAT TODAY EITHER!

27

39

*IT'S OBVIOUS THAT MR. BARTHOLOMEW IS CONFUSED. THERE'S NO FRYING PAN OR FIRE ANYWHERE NEAR HIM.

I WAS PICKED UP BY THE SECOND PELICAN-WHALER AND STUCK IN THE NEXT CELL.

DO YOU KNOW WHERE WE ARE, MR. BARTHOLOMEW?

BAH! IN A SUSPENDED CASTLE.

YEP, SUSPENDED.

SUSPENDED? SUSPENDED FROM WHAT?

FROM NOTHING.

OH, MY GOODNESS. I WAS SO HAPPY ON THE "A"...

TAP! TAP! TAP! TAP! TAP! TAP!

FOOTSTEPS!

LET ME STAND ON YOUR SHOULDERS. QUICK!

CLINK! CLINK!

CREAK

OOF! FFF! PFT!

WHAT'S THIS?! THE PRISONER HAS...

PHIL! ARE YOU OK?

I'M OK.

HURRY! TAKE HIS KEYS, MR. BARTHOLOMEW!

29

41

CLIMB UP, MY FRIENDS. CLIMB UP AND DO YOUR JOB!

THE LADDER! BRING THE LADDER!

THE PROPHETS PREDICTED IT: "FROM OUT OF THE WHALE-GALLEY WILL COME THE CUTTERS OF THE ROPE..."

?

AND YOU'RE THE ONES!

BRAVO!

REALLY, MY FRIEND...

LET ME EMBRACE YOU!

GLORY TO THE CUTTERS OF THE ROPE!

COULD YOU PLEASE EXPLAIN WHAT YOU MEAN?

HE'S RIGHT. WE NEED TO EXPLAIN IT TO THEM.

NO, YOU DO IT BETTER.

GO AHEAD AND TELL THEM.

OH, YOU'RE JUST SAYING THAT TO MAKE ME HAPPY.

I DON'T KNOW HOW TO TELL A STORY.

OK... A LONG TIME AGO—A VERY LONG TIME AGO...2,327 YEARS AGO, TO BE PRECISE—OUR PEOPLE WERE THE VICTIMS OF A CURSE... IT'S SO HARD TO TALK ABOUT IT...

HE CAN REALLY TELL A STORY!

VERY HARD!

IT'S ALL SO SAD.

SNIFF! SNIFF!

...WE HAVE BEEN CONDEMNED TO LIVE IN THIS SUSPENDED CASTLE UNTIL THE DAY THE ROPE IS CUT...

...BY TWO STRANGERS WHO COME OUT OF A WHALE-GALLEY.

THAT'S WHY WE'VE BEEN HUNTING FOR CENTURIES AND CENTURIES...

EATING WHALE-GALLEY IS OK FOR A WHILE, BUT...

YUCK!

UP TO NOW, NO PRISONER HAS EVER DARED TO REVOLT...

YOU'RE THE FIRST!

YOU ARE THE CUTTERS OF THE ROPE!

LONG LIVE OUR SAVIORS!

BRAVO!

Down the well, in a world of utter fantasy...

Frédéric Othon Aristidès (1931-2013), known as Fred, was of France's most influential and revered cartoonists. In the sixties, he co-founded *Hara-Kiri*, the leading satirical publication of the May '68 movement and the predecessor of *Charlie Hebdo*. *Philémon*, his story for young readers and his most celebrated creation, was first published in *Pilote* in 1965 by René Goscinny, the author of *Astérix*. Millions of French people have grown up with it, and it has inspired many of today's most talented cartoonists.

Fred was born in Paris to a Greek immigrant family. The young Fred grew up hearing nightly stories from his mother, inspired by Greek mythology, French fairy tales, and the British literature she herself had grown up with. He kept the habit all his life: every night as he drifted to sleep, he gave himself a few unrelated words (such as whale, owl, or galley ship) and built a story around it. While there's no knowing where exactly he found his inspiration, he said he often got his best ideas while taking a bath. In the following pages, we reference some of the sources of his fertile imagination.

Whaling

The hunting of whales has existed for thousands of years. Whales, which are mammals (not fish), have been hunted for their meat and their oil, which was used to light lamps before the discovery of electricity. People also used to harvest whale's baleen (also referred to as "whalebone") to make corset boning, collar stiffeners, parasol ribs, and paper-folders. Whales were usually killed by harpoons, which were shot or thrown from boats. In 1851, Herman Melville, an American author who had been a sailor, published his masterpiece, *Moby Dick*, about a captain's quest to kill a great white whale. By the late 1930s, more than fifty thousand whales were killed each year. There is much debate today as to whether whales should still be hunted.

A whaler with a collection of baleen.

"Pieces of cleaned baleen," ca. 1900, Alaska State Library, Rev. Samuel Spriggs Photograph Collection.

One of the first submersible boats, known as The Drebbel, *was built by Cornelius Drebbel in 1620. It looked like a whale and was powered by oars.*

Pieter Lastman, "Jonah and the Whale," 1621.

Jonah and the Whale

Jonah is a prophet who appears in the Old Testament of the Bible and in several sections of the Qur'an. According to religious texts, Jonah disobeyed God's command to alert the people of Nineveh, capital of Assyria, that they were to be destroyed because of their wickedness. Jonah fled by ship but was thrown overboard by the sailors in a storm. He was swallowed by a whale or a giant fish (depending on the translation) and spent three days and nights inside it before being spat out.

Galleys

A galley in Asterix the Gladiator, *originally published in* Pilote, *the same magazine that published* Philemon.

Galleys are wooden ships that are propelled by rowers. They were used for trade and warfare in the Mediterranean Sea as long as three thousand years ago. Some had one row of rowers (monoremes), some had two (biremes), and some had three (triremes). Galleys often had drummers to help rowers keep a steady pace. Rowers allowed the ships to move against the current or even when there was no wind. Of course, rowers took up a great deal of space, and a lot of food had to be kept on board to feed them. This made them impractical for long, ocean-going voyages. It was not unusual to sentence criminals to galley service, and "galley slaves" were sometimes even enlisted from captives and prisoners of war. Galleys were still used for warfare, trade, and piracy as late as the nineteenth century.

A Cretan galley from Theseus and the Minotaur by Yvan Pommaux, another TOON Graphic.

A still from Orson Welles's 1962 film adaptation of The Trial.

The Trial

In *The Trial* by Franz Kafka, a German-speaking Czech author, a man is arrested and put on trial for a crime that is never revealed to him or the reader. This is similar to the way Philemon and Bartholomew are put to work in the whale-galley but have no idea where they are going.

171. PARIS — Station du Métropolitain - Place de la Bastille

Magasins Réunis

The Paris Métro

T he first line of the
Paris subway, or
Métropolitain,
opened in 1900, during
the World's Fair. Many
of the entrances still have
the flowery Art Nouveau ironwork designed by the architect
Hector Guimard. There are now sixteen lines with 303 stations,
including the largest one in the world, *Châtelet-Les Halles,*
and the Métro carries more than four million passengers a
day. Métro stations used to have heavy gates called *portillons*–
pictured above and in this book–to keep people from getting
hurt as they rushed to trains that were about to close their
doors and zoom off. Since 2000, several lines have become
entirely automated and driverless. On those lines, the train
enters the station in a glass tube whose doors line up to those
of the cars and open when the train is in place. One can only
imagine what Fred would have made of that design if he had
been writing today.

Opened doors on the glass tube of
the automated Number Fourteen
line of the Paris Métro.

Lighthouses

The earliest lighthouses were constructed in ancient times, before the third century BCE. Although they were initially lit by fires (instead of lamps), the purpose was the same: to guide ships in a dark ocean. Today, the use of lighthouses has declined due to replacement by modern electronic navigational systems. Fred's owl-lighthouse takes the idea of "guiding sailors across the ocean" more literally, however, allowing seafarers to walk on the beams of light themselves!

The Old Lady Lighthouse in Brittany, France, built in 1887, housed a keeper until it was automated in 1995.

Castles in the Air

Suspended, flying, or floating castles (or cities) are now a common theme in science fiction and fantasy. Floating islands appear in Homer's *Odyssey* and in Jonathan Swift's 1726 satirical novel, *Gulliver's Travels*, in which the hero visits a floating island city called Laputa. Laputa appears in the Japanese title of Hayao Miyazaki's 1986 animated film *The Castle in the Sky*. Fred's book precedes Miyazaki's work and may have provided inspiration, just as Fred himself may have seen *The Castle of the Pyrenees*, a 1959 painting by Belgian Surrealist René Magritte, in which a castle on a boulder defies gravity over a stormy ocean.

Top left: The Castle of the Pyrenees, *1959, a painting by Belgian Surrealist painter René Magritte.* Above: *Publicity still from the film* Laputa: The Castle in the Sky *by Hayao Miyazaki, 1986.* Left: *J.J. Grandville, Illustration of Laputa from* Gulliver's Travels, *1838.*

Tips for Parents, Teachers, and Librarians:
TOON GRAPHICS FOR VISUAL READERS

TOON Graphics are comics and visual narratives that bring the text to life in a way that captures young readers' imaginations and makes them want to read on—and read more. When the authors are also artists, they can convey their creative vision with pictures as well as words. They can enhance the overarching theme and present important details that are absorbed by the reader along with the text. Young readers also develop their aesthetic sense when they experience the relationship of text to picture in all its communicative power.

Reading TOON Graphics is a pleasure for all. Beginners and seasoned readers alike will sharpen both their literal and inferential reading skills.

Let the pictures tell the story

The very economy of comic books necessitates the use of a reader's imaginative powers. In comics, the images often imply rather than tell outright. Readers must learn to make connections between events to complete the narrative, helping them build their ability to visualize and to make "mental maps."

A comic book also gives readers a great deal of visual context that can be used to investigate the thinking behind the characters' choices.

Pay attention to the artist's choices

Look carefully at the artwork: it offers a subtext that at first is sensed only on a subliminal level by the reader and encourages rereading. It creates a sense of continuity for the action, and it can tell you about the art, architecture, and clothing of a specific time period. It may present the atmosphere, landscape, and flora and fauna of another time or of another part of the world. TOON Graphics can also present

multiple points of view and simultaneous events in a manner not permitted by linear written narration. Facial expressions and body language reveal subtle aspects of characters' personalities beyond what can be expressed by words.

Read and reread!

Readers can compare comic book artists' styles and evaluate how different authors get their point across in different ways. In investigating the author's choices, a young reader begins to gain a sense of how all literary and art forms can be used to convey the author's central ideas.

The world of TOON Graphics and of comic book art is rich and varied. Making meaning out of reading with the aid of visuals may be the best way to become a lifelong reader, one who knows how to read for pleasure and for information—a reader who *loves* to read.

COLLECT THEM ALL!

Set of 6 Hardcover Books ISBN: 978-1-61479-497-4

Hardcover Book ISBN
978-1-61479-498-1

Hardcover Book ISBN
978-1-61479-501-8

Hardcover Book ISBN
978-1-61479-503-2

Hardcover Book ISBN
978-1-61479-499-8

Hardcover Book ISBN
978-1-61479-500-1

Hardcover Book ISBN
978-1-61479-502-5